Anonymous

The Thousand Islands

the summer paradise of the St. Lawrence River

Anonymous

The Thousand Islands
the summer paradise of the St. Lawrence River

ISBN/EAN: 9783337302221

Printed in Europe, USA, Canada, Australia, Japan

Cover: Foto ©Andreas Hilbeck / pixelio.de

More available books at **www.hansebooks.com**

The

Thousand Islands,

THE SUMMER PARADISE OF THE

ST. LAWRENCE RIVER.

Y ONE WHO HAS BEEN THERE.

WATERTOWN, N. Y.:
TIMES AND REFORMER PRINTING AND PUBLISHING HOUSE.
1885.

"And they were happy, and well content, sailing the way the river went."

THE THOUSAND ISLES.

BY HON. CALEB LYON.

THE Thousand Isles, The Thousand Isles,
Dimpled the wave around them smiles.
Kissed by a thousand red-lipped flowers,
Gemmed by a thousand emerald bowers,
A thousand birds their praises wake,
By rocky glade and plumy brake,
A thousand cedars' fragant shade
Falls where the Indians' children played,
And fancy's dream my heart beguiles
While singing thee, The Thousand Isles.

The flag of France first o'er them hung,
The mass was said, the vespers sung.
The friars of Jesus hailed the strands,
As Blessed Virgin Mary's lands,
The red men mutely heard, surprised,
Their heathen names all christianized.
Next floated a banner with cross and crown,
'Twas freedom's eagle plucked it down,
Retaining its pure and crimson dyes
With stars of their own their native skies.

There St. Lawrence gentlest flows,
There the south wind softest blows,
There the lilies whitest bloom.
There the birch has leafiest gloom,
There the red deer feed in Spring,
There doth glitter wood-duck's wing,
There leap the muskallonge at morn,
There the loon's night song is borne,
There is the fisherman's paradise,
With trolling-skiff at red sunrise.

The Thousand Isles, The Thousand Isles,
Their charm from every care beguiles.
Titian alone hath grace to paint
The triumph of their patron saint,
Whose waves return on Memory's tide;
LaSalle and Piquet, side by side
Proud Frontenac and bold Champlain,
There act their wanderings o'er again;
And while their golden sunlight smiles,
Pilgrims shall greet thee, Thousand Isles.

FISHING PARTIES AT FROST ISLAND.

A SUMMER PARADISE.

THE THOUSAND ISLANDS.

Nature nowhere presents more alluring charms than in that labyrinth of land and water, rock and tree, known as The Thousand Islands of the St. Lawrence River, and nowhere else, during our sultry summers can pleasure and health seekers find the objects sought in larger measure.

HISTORICAL.

RESORT OF THE RED MAN.

This region has a history which is full of romantic interest. When it was first discovered by Europeans, they found it a favorite resort of the red men, who called it Manatoana, or Garden of the Great Spirit, because of the abundant fish and game. Their tents were seen dotting the islands and shores, and their canoes darting to and fro along the river.

EARLY EXPLORERS AND ACCOUNTS.

The river was discovered August 10, 1535, by Jacques Cartier, who named it St. Lawrence in honor of the saint whose feast is celebrated on that day. The first European who visited Lake Ontario was Samuel Champlain, in 1615; and in his meagre descriptions he mentions some beautiful and very large islands at the beginning of the St. Lawrence. It is supposed that some French explorers, who went up the river about 1650, gave the region its present name, "*Milles Isles,*" or Thousand Islands. In the papers relating to De Comceile's and De Tracy's expeditions against the Mohawk Indians in 1666, the islands are complained of as obstructing navigation and mystifying the most experienced Iroquois pilots.

In the year 1620 a Capt. Ponchot described the region somewhat minutely in his journal, which was afterwards published in Switz-

erland, and there have been frequent allusions to, and descriptions of it, written and published from that time to the present. The picturesque scenery of this spot also seems to
have made a lasting impression upon French artists, as one of the finest paintings that greet
the eye of an American on entering the Picture Gallery at Versailles, presents a view of
these attractive wilds.

IN ROMANCE AND SONG.

We find them occasionally in the poetry and fiction of this latter period. The "Canadian Boat Song," by the great Irish poet, Thomas Moore, commencing:

> "Faintly as tolls the evening chime
> Our voices keep tune and our oars keep time,"

was written in 1804, it is said, on Hart's Island, opposite The Crossmon. During their pass-
age down the river James Fennimore Cooper and Washington Irving visited the Thousand

Islands, and were fascinated by them.
Cooper makes them the scene of some
of the most interesting incidents of
"The Pathfinder," from which we
copy the following:

"By sunset again the cutter was up
with the first of the islands that lie in
the outlet of the lake, and ere it was
dark she was running through the narrow channels on her way to the long-
sought station. At 9 o'clock, however, Cap. insisted that they should
anchor, as the maze of islands became
so complicated and obscure, that he
feared, at every opening, the party
would find themselves under the guns
of a French fort. * * * The islands
might not have been literally a thous-
and in number, but they were so nu-

IN CANADIAN WATERS.   merous and small as to baffle calcu-
lation, though occasionally one of a larger size than common was passed. Jasper had
quitted what might have been termed the main channel, and was wending his way, with a
good stiff breeze and a favorable current, through passes that were sometimes so narrow
that there appeared to be barely room sufficient for the Scud's spars to clear the trees; at
other moments he shot across little bays, and buried the cutter again amid rocks, forest and
bushes. The water was so transparent that there was no occasion for the lead, and being
of very equal depth, little risk was actually run."

Farther on he describes the island where "The Pathfinder" and his party secreted
themselves, which is so good of many others that we insert it here:

LITTLE LEHIGH ISLAND.

"Lying in the midst of twenty others, it was not an easy matter to find it, since boats might pass quite near, and, by the glimpses caught through the openings, this particular island would be taken for a part of some other. Indeed, the channels between the islands that lay around the one we have been describing, were so narrow that it was even difficult to say which portions of the land were connected, or which separated, even as one stood in their center, with the express desire of ascertaining the truth. The little bay, in particular, that Jasper used as a harbor, was so embowered with bushes and shut in with islands, that the sails of the cutter being lowered, her own people, on one occasion, had searched for hours before they could find the Scud, on their return from a short excursion among the adjacent channels in quest of fish."

IN THE PRESENT.

"Now, however, the inexorably rotating kaleidoscope of time has shaken away the savage scenes of old, never to be repeated, and new ones appear to the eye of the present. No longer in Alexandria Bay—fortunately still beautiful—does Nature reign in silent majesty, for the constant flutter and bustle of the life and gayety of a summer resort have superseded her. But although Alexandria Bay is in the continual tumult of life, for some fortunate and almost unaccountable reason, the Thousand Islands are not in the least tinctured with the *blasé* air of an ordinary watering-place, nor are they likely to become so. There are hundreds, thousands of places, rugged and solitary, among which a boat can glide, while its occupant lies gloriously indolent, doing nothing but reveling in the realization of life; little bays, almost land-locked, where the resinous odors of hemlock and pine fill the nostrils, and the whispers of Nature's unseen life seem but to make the solitude more perceptible. Sometimes the vociferous cawing of crows sounds through the hollow woods, or a solitary eagle lifts from his perch on the top of a stark and dead pine, and sails majestically across the blue arch of the sky. Such scenes occur on a beautiful sheet of water called Lake of the Isle, lying placidly and balmily in the lap of the piney hills of Wells Island, reflecting their rugged crests in its glassy surface, dotted here and there by tiny islands. In the stillest bays are spots that seem to lie in a Rip Van Winkle sleep, where one would scarcely be surprised to see an Indian canoe shoot from beneath the hemlocks of the shore into the open, freighted with a Natty Bumpo or a Chingachgook, breaking the placid surface of the water into slowly widening ripples. In such a spot, one evening after a day spent in sketching, when pad-

dling our boat about in an indolent, aimless way, looking down through the crystal clearness of the water to the jangle of weeds below, now frightening a pickerel from his haunt or starting a brood of wood duck from among the rushes and arrow-heads, we found ourselves belated. As the sun set in a blaze of crimson and gold, two boatmen moving homeward passed darkly along the glassy surface that caught the blazing light of the sky, and across the water came, in measured rythm with the dip of their oars, the tune of a quaint old half-melancholy Methodist hymn that they sang. We listened as the song trailed after them, until they turned into an inlet behind the dusky woods and were lost to view. From such romantic and secluded recesses, one can watch the bustle and hurry of life as serenely as though one were the inhabitant of another planet."

IN RECENT LITERATURE.

During the past few years wherein the Thousand Islands have suddenly become one of the leading resorts for summer recreation, they have been prominent in the current literature and pictorial illustrations of the country. Newspapers and magazines have made them the subject of many long and in-

SAFE POINT.

teresting articles; reporters, essayists, romancers, poets and humorists have seemed to vie with each other in calling the attention of the public to this place of enchantment; and the consequence is that a vast and annually swelling tide of humanity flows that way, and many linger there from early June until late October.

DESCENDING THE RAPIDS.

Fair St. Lawrence! What poet has sung of its grace
As it sleeps in the sun, with its smile-dimpled face
Beaming up to the sky that it mirrors? What brush
Has e'er pictured the charm of the marvelous hush
Of its silence, or caught the warm glow of its tints
As the afternoon wanes, and the even-star glints
In its beautiful depths? And what pen shall betray
The sweet secrets that hide from man's vision away
In its solitudes wild? 'Tis the river of dreams;
You may float in your boat on the bloom-bordered streams,
Where its islands like emeralds matchless are set,
And forget that you live, and as quickly forget
That they die in that world you have left; for the calm
Of content is within you, the blessing of balm
Is upon you forever.—ANON.

FIDDLER'S ELBOW.

ITEMS OF INTEREST.

We have stated that the St. Lawrence was discovered and named in 1535, and that Lake Ontario was discovered in 1615. A few other references to the past may be interesting. The first military post on Lake Ontario and the upper St. Lawrence was Fort Frontenac, which was established by the French under the direction of Count ˙de Frontenac, in 1673, on the spot where Kingston now stands. During the French war in 1758, this post was captured by an English army of 3,340 men, commanded by Colonel John Bradstreet, who crossed over from Oswego. It then remained in British possession until surrendered again to the French, in whose possession it remained until a short time before the Revolution.

Fort Carleton, the ruins of which are seen upon the upper end of Carleton Island, just below Cape Vincent, was built under the direction of Gen. Carleton, as a British post, in 1777. During the Revolutionary war, and for some time afterwards, it was the principal military station on the lake. It was finally abandoned as a place of military defense in 1808. It remained in nominal possession of the British until the beginning of the war of 1812.

The boundary line between Canada and the United States was definitely settled in 1822. The first steamboat appeared on Lake Ontario and the St. Lawrence in 1817, causing great excitement and demonstration among the people along the shores. Its name was the Oneida.

In 1823 all the islands in the state between Ogdensburg, on the St. Lawrence, and Grindstone Island, in Lake Ontario, were granted to Elisha Camp of Sackets Harbor, and all titles within these limits must be traced to this proprietor. The Patriot War, which led to exciting military scenes and adventures on the St. Lawrence, occurred in 1837-39. The British steamer "Sir Robert Peel" was fired and burnt on the south side of Wells Island, on the night of May 29-30, 1838, and the "Battle of the Windmill" occurred at Prescott in November of the same year, a memorable battle to the elder Crossmon, who was taken prisoner during the engagement, tried and sentenced to be shot. Owing to his extreme youth a respite was obtained, and he was afterwards ransomed, thus barely escaping with his life.

THE WINDMILL.

GEOLOGICAL.

The geological formation of the Thousand Islands is mostly gniess rock of the Laurentian period. The rock is composed largely of a reddish feldspar, with mixtures of quartz and hornblende, and a little magnetic iron ore. There are also occasionally thin veins of trap and greenstone, and in places a variety of crystalline mineral forms. Potsdam sandstone occurs among the islands in thick masses, rising sometimes into high cliffs. Before reaching Brockville from above, and for a long distance below, a calciferous sandstone and the older limestones constitute the only rock, and in these are found the organic remains of lower forms of animal and vegetable life.

DRIED GRASSES FROM THE ISLANDS.

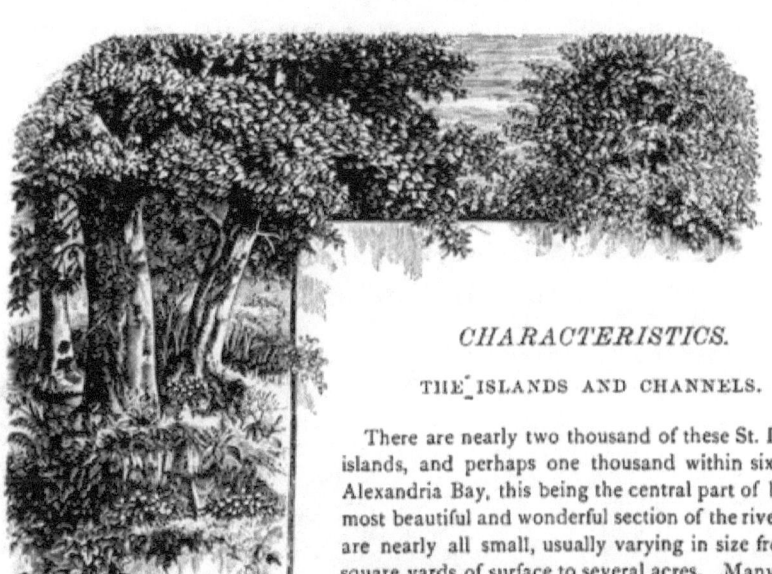

CHARACTERISTICS.

THE ISLANDS AND CHANNELS.

There are nearly two thousand of these St. Lawrence islands, and perhaps one thousand within six miles of Alexandria Bay, this being the central part of by far the most beautiful and wonderful section of the river. They are nearly all small, usually varying in size from a few square yards of surface to several acres. Many of them are separated only by narrow channels, which are generally deep, but sometimes shallow. Quiet and inviting little bays are found here and there. All the islands are thickly studded with trees of rich foliage, but generally of moderate or stunted growth, many of which stand close to the water's edge, and afford cooling shade to passing boatmen. In the bays and by the sides of the islands is excellent fishing, bass and pickerel being the principal fish, but the famous muskallonge is sufficiently numerous to warrant the fisherman in expecting an electric bite from him at any moment, which will put his strength and skill to their utmost test.

WELLS ISLAND.

Special mention should here be made of the largest of the islands, the lower end of which is just below the village of Alexandria Bay. It is eight miles long, and from a few feet to four miles wide. Portions of it have been cultivated as farms for the last half a century. Other parts are charmingly wooded, and some of its rock features are exceedingly picturesque. The lower portion is separated into two parts by the "Lake of the Island," which is connected with the river on the American and Canadian sides by two narrow channels. This quiet lake, three or four miles long, is fringed with rich foliage and occasional bold rocks, and is a favorite fishing and hunting resort.

AS A SUMMER RESORT.

OLD TIMES.

Not until 1872 was the attention of the general public turned to the Thousand Islands as a "watering-place," or resort for pleasure seekers and invalids, although some discerning

INLET TO THE RIFF.

ones had been in the habit of spending a few summer days or weeks there for more than a quarter of a century previous. There Governor Seward shook hands across the party chasm with Silas Wright, and caught bass and muskallonge with him from the same boat, exchanging practical quotations and cheerful jokes instead of political opinions and arguments. There Rev. Dr. Geo. Bethune dropped theology, and Gen. Dick Taylor forgot military tactics, and floated sociably together down among the islands. The wily Martin Van Buren, his witty son John, Frank Blair, and other politicians of the old school, found respite from the affairs of State and partisan squabbles, and were soothed and softened by the influences of nature. And when these intellectual giants returned from their fishing expeditions they found rare good cheer and comfort in the unpretentious old Crossmon House at the Bay, where the elder Crossmon was then known as the prince of country landlords, and in such goodly company learned thoroughly the fine art of managing and entertaining guests.

THE NEW DEPARTURE.

In the summer of 1872 two or three things occurred opportunely to draw immediate attention to the river attractions. George W. Pullman, the palace-car king, had become enamored with the place, purchased a beautiful island nearly opposite the Bay, and erected thereon suitable buildings for a luxurious summer residence. By his invitation, in 1872, Gen. Grant and family and a party of friends went to Pullman's Island, as his guests, and remained eight days. The same season a large party of New York and Southern editors made an excursion to the islands, and dined *al fresco* on the same island, the viands being furnished from the cuisine of the Crossmon House. These two events brought the islands to the notice of the people in all parts of the country.

CATCHING MUSKALLONGE.

So when the big new hotels were opened in the summer of 1873, the people at once began to hasten to them, and since then they have continued to come every year in large numbers. About the same time there began to be a great demand for islands on which to build summer cottages. A large number were sold in 1872 and '73, and the demand and sale have continued each year since. Of course the best of the islands have now been appropriated, but there are many desirable ones left, and beautiful points also on the main shore and on Wells Island.

DISTINGUISHED GUESTS.

The Crossmon has been particularly honored of late by being the chosen stopping-place of President Arthur, Gen. Sheridan, Cardinal McCloskey and Herbert Spencer.

FISHING PICNICS.

Several of these enjoyable affairs come off every pleasant day. A party of from ten to twenty-five ladies and gentlemen set off in a steam yacht for some distant fishing-ground, taking liberal supplies from the hotel, and about half as many oarsmen as excursionists.

Each oarsman takes his own skiff and fishing tackle. The boats being towed in single file behind the yacht, present the appearance of some strange marine animal with a very long tail. An island is selected as the base of operations, and here the yacht is moored to the shore and the party separates, each skiff with its two or three occupants taking a different direction, with the understanding to meet again at that island for dinner. At the appointed hour the boats return, and the oarsmen nearly all of whom are good cooks, set at work preparing dinner. A fireplace is quickly improvised out of rocks, and the savory odors of a hot dinner soon mingle with the piney odors of the woods. The yacht carries boards for tables and the island supplies rocks to support them. The afternoon is spent in rambles on the adjacent islands, or in story-telling under some big tree, while two or three drowsy gentlemen go off to sleep under the influence of the fresh air and a hearty dinner. Frequenters of the islands often bring hammocks with them for these occasions.

PICNIC DINNER ON AN ISLAND.

ISLAND ROYAL.

PARTICULAR ISLANDS.

Island Royal, owned by Mr. Royal E. Deane, of New York, is situated opposite Point Vivian, two miles from Alexandria Bay, and quite near Wells Island. The veranda of the cottage is twenty feet above the water, and from this elevation a view unsurpassed upon the channel may be enjoyed. Many of the river captains pass within hailing distance of this beautiful spot. Mr. Deane and family for many years have been summer residents upon the river.

Just above the village in the American channel, is Warner Island, owned by H. H. Warner, of Rochester, who is famous for the magnitude, boldness and success of his business operations. The line steamers pass within a few feet of his cottage. The river-bound half-acre on which it stands commands one of the most extensive views among the islands. Mr. Warner and family are in the habit of remaining here two or three months of the year, and their gracious hospitalities have won them hosts of friends among the frequenters of the Thousand Islands.

We have already referred to Pullman's island.

WARNER ISLAND, AS SEEN FROM WELLS' ISLAND.

Near by is Nobby, which, owing to its position and natural formation is one of the most desirable among the islands. The owner H. R. Heath, of New York has devoted

NOBBY ISLAND.

much time and capital in improvements both on Nobby and the famous Oven which is also in his posession.

Rye Island has recently been purchased by Nathaniel W. Hunt, of Brooklyn, and re-christened St. Elmo. The island is a prominent one, and as the cottage to be built upon it is the design of the architect who has built most of the finest cottages on the river it is fair to presume that St. Elmo will not be behind her sisters in architectural beauty.

A few rods from The Crossmon, between it and Well's Island, is Hart's Island, a little paradise, with one of the largest of the island cottages.

Mrs. H. G. LeConte, of Philadelphia, Pa., has recently purchased Isle Imperial, just above Hart's Island, much enlarged it by piering and filling in, and erected a cottage costing about $20,000.

Plantagent Island was purchased by Judge Charles Donohue, of New York, and re-christened "St. John." He has built a handsome cottage upon it and is constantly making improvements.

The details might be indefinitely extended.

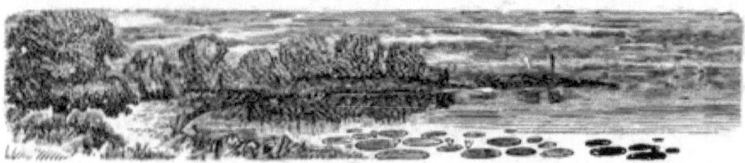

A short distance down the river from the Bay is a triplet of charming little islands. They are : Little Lehigh, owned by Chas. H. Cummings, of New York; Sport, owned by Mrs. H. E. Packer of Mauch Chunk, Pa., and E. P. Wilbur, Bethlehem, Pa., and Idlewild, owned by Mrs. R. A. Packer, of Sayre, Pa. The first two are connected by a handsome wrought iron bridge.

Sport Island is nicely terraced, and a private gas house furnishes the means of illuminating it at night with two hundred lights.

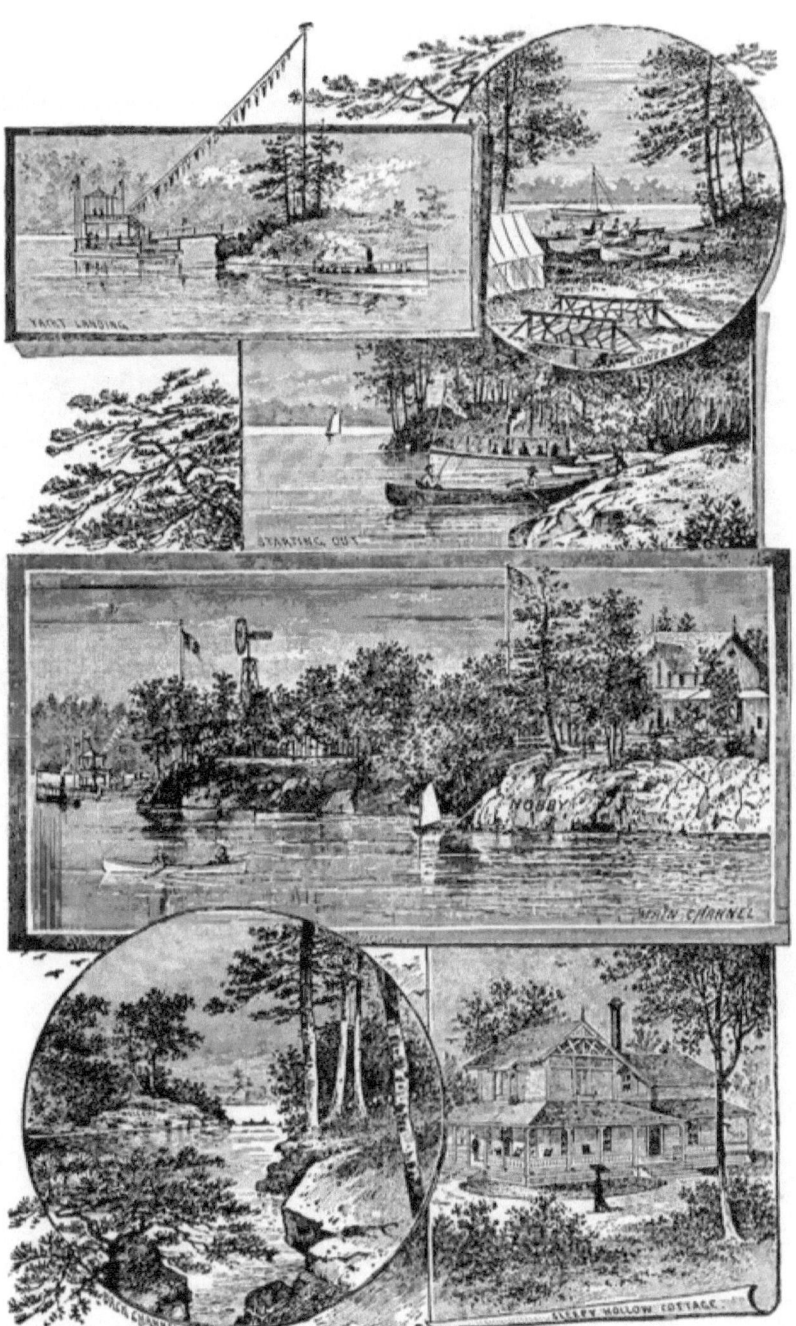

GLIMPSES OF NOBBY ISLAND.

THE CAPES.

Many small capes which scallop the main shores of the river, afford beautiful building sites, and some of them are adorned by handsome cottages.   The demand for these capes has increased of late, and it is probable that before many years the shores for a long distance each way from the Bay, as well as the islands, will be thickly studded with cottages, owned by health and pleasure seekers from abroad.

Perhaps the most desirable point on the river was purchased by Dr. J. G. Holland, the celebrated author, and late editor of The Century.   It is at the mouth of the lovely little bay overlooked by The Crossmon, and only a few rods across the water from it.   Dr. Holland has expended many thousands of dollars in erecting here a luxurious cottage and im-

DR. J. G. HOLLAND'S LATE RESIDENCE, "BONNIE CASTLE."

proving the grounds.   The point is named "Bonnie Castle," from one of Dr. Holland's novels.   The family are in the habit of spending three to four months of the year on this island, and here Dr. Holland did much of his literary work

SOME NAMES EXPLAINED.

The historically famous Devil's Oven is an island so named from a water cave into which a boat can be rowed from the river.   This cave was the hiding place for many months of the famous "Bill Johnson" during the Patriot War of 1837–39.   Aided and sustained by his daughter Kate, he finally escaped.

Goose Bay is a well known fishing and hunting ground three miles from the village.   Eel Bay is another at the head of Wells Island.   Halsteads Bay is another on the Canadian side.

Fiddler's Elbow is a thick and favorite cluster of islands in the Canadian waters.

The Riff is the long narrow inlet to the Lake of the Islands over a mile long, and is so narrow that a child can throw a stone across it at any point, and yet is navigable for small yachts.

OVEN ISLAND.

THE COTTAGES.

The river cottages are numerous a n d every year important additions are made to them. It is notice-able that as time passes the new ones constructed are made more and more ele-gant and improved.

PARKS.

The Thousand Island Park of the Methodists is on the upper end of Wells Island, seven miles from Alexandria Bay. It was started in 1873. and to its natural beau-ties have been added delightful drives and walks; a village of cottages, bath houses, and buildings for religious purposes and the accommodation of visitors. Here are held Sunday school, temperance and educational conventions every season.

Round Island Park, two miles above Thousand Island Park, belongs to a Baptist As-sociation which was organized in the summer of 1879. It occupies the whole of a large island.

Prospect Park is yet farther up the river, on a high wooded point on the main shore, and is laid out in streets and lots, many of which are occupied.

Westminster Park is at the foot of Wells Island about a mile and a half from the Bay. It was purchased in 1874 by a Presbyterian stock company, and has been rapidly improved, having now several miles of drives, and some fine buildings. In the midst of the ground is a high hill, to the top of which is a winding roadway. This hill is called Mt. Beulah, and is surmounted by a pentagonal chapel, which will accommodate one thousand persons, and has a tower 136 feet high, presenting one of the best views of the river and islands.

These parks are connected with each other and the Bay many times daily by steamers, which afford delightful little trips.

Although the Thousand Islands are now dotted with cottages and thronged here and there with people, their original wild beauty and enticements remain, the trees and rocks ; the majestic flow of crystal pure waters ; the yet purer air, with its splendid tonic and heal-

ing proper-
ties; the
ever vary-
ing views;
the oppor-
tunities for
boating,
fishing,
hunting,
bathing,
etc.; all are
here, and
man has ad-
ded to them
yet more.

RIVER SPORTS.

Boating, fishing, hunting, cruising among the islands in row boats or steam yachts, visiting many points of historical or traditionary interest, pic-nicing in large or small parties, open-air feasting, and lounging under the trees by the water's edge, are terms which sum up the principal sports of the river. There are many small boats at the Bay, and many good oarsmen stand ready to serve at a moderate price, those who want their services. These oarsmen are a convenience, but not a necessity, to the enjoyments among the islands. They know all the good fishing grounds, can give all needed instruction in the art of catching, will furnish the requisite fishing tackle, and cook the fish in dainty and appetizing style when caught.

Black bass and pickerel, large and gamy, abound in these waters—many muskallonge are also caught every season, and the lady or gentleman who hooks and secures one or more of these largest and best of all fresh water fish, becomes the heroine or hero of the day on returning to the Bay.

Ladies are often the lucky ones, and sometimes pull in a muskallonge of enormous size, courageously refusing the while all masculine assistance.

Occasionally a muskallonge weighs as high as forty pounds, a pickerel as high as twenty pounds, and a bass as high as six or seven pounds. The muskallonge are mostly taken between the middle of May and the last of July; the bass bite best between the middle of June and September, while the pickerel are caught early and late in the season, and all the season.

Trolling is the usual and most exciting method of fishing among the islands, though much pleasant still fishing is also done.

"WILD FLOWERS OF THE ISLANDS."

Late fall and early spring, as all hunters know, are the times for shooting duck, when they flock to the bays and coves of this section of the river, by thousands. It is not unusual for a fishing party to return to the Bay at night with a hundred or more fine fish, nor for the hunter to come in with fifteen or twenty broadbilled trophies of his marksmanship.

STEAMERS AND YACHTS.

The large line steamers are seen plying up and down the river at frequent intervals. All of them touch at the Bay, and many others nearly as large are devoted to excursions. A new company has been formed to meet the demands and necessities of the increasing travel along the River and Lake Ontario, by putting on a line of floating palaces, similar to those on the Hudson, and costing from $80,000 to $100,000 each.

An important feature of life at the Bay, and among the Thousand Islands, is the great and increasing number of steam yachts, large and small, which glide to and fro over the blue waters, and in and out among the island channels, during the pleasure season Some of these are models of architectural beauty, such as can be seen almost nowhere else. In going considerable distances on the river, up and down and across from shore to shore, and island to island, and point to point, when fishing is not desired, these yachts have nearly superceded the row boats, although the latter are always ready, with good oarsmen, when required. These yachts afford a swift and delightful conveyance for small parties, as the larger steamers do for larger parties, and for distant places and pic-nics, or extensive views of the river scenery.

THE WANDERER.

The best way of gaining a comprehensive idea of the magnitude and wildness of this archipelago is by taking a trip on the Island Wanderer. This fast steamer makes two trips daily of forty miles each, taking in on its way some of the most intricate channels among the islands.

A SCENE OF ENCHANTMENT.

The summer night scenes at the Bay are wierdly enchanting, and European travelers say they remind them of the night scenes at Venice, and are quite as beautiful. The illuminations extend far up and down the river, on gliding yachts, and steamers, on the islands, along the grounds, and in the windows and towers of the great hotels, and added to these are the lights of the village, and almost nightly displays of Chinese lanterns, Roman candles, rockets and other fireworks. This superb kaleidoscope of river fires must be witnessed to be appreciated.

THE RIFF.

IMPORTANT EFFECTS.

An ardent admirer of the Thousand Islands has said that they were conducive to four important effects: health, happiness, enthusiasm and love. Concerning this last it should be said that cupid is all powerful here. The momentous question which is the key of matrimony has been asked and answered many scores of times among these charming islands.

ALEXANDRIA BAY.

This village is the central point of interest from its nearness to the most picturesque part of the islands. It has a population of about seven hundred, and is prettily situated on a point of land between two river bays making it almost water bound. The fishing in this vicinity is better than elsewhere owing to the greater number of islands which cause quiet shallows where fish delight to congregate. Here to is the

CHURCH OF THE THOUSAND ISLANDS,

built in 1851 through the instrumentality of Rev. Dr. George W. Bethune, of the Reformed Dutch Church, who was a regular visitor at the Bay for many successive years, commencing as early as 1845. The church building, which is a chaste stone structure, with truncated tower, stands on a knoll in the edge of the village.

METHODIST CHURCH.

There is also a pretty little church recently completed by the Methodists at a cost of about $6,000, finished inside in black walnut and ash, and nicely carpeted. It has a capacity for seating about 300 persons.

PROSPECTIVE EPISCOPAL CHURCH.

Bishop Huntington and others are making an effort to secure the erection of an Episcopal Chapel at the Bay, and a part of the necessary funds have been pledged and collected.

LIBRARY.

A fine library has been established at the Bay for the use of visitors, under the auspices of the Y. M. C. A. It has about one thousand volumes, a large portion of which were generously donated by its founder, Dr. Holland. These will be increased from year to year.

THE CROSSMON.

THE OLD AND NEW.

We now come to that which provides sweet and invigorating rest after the varied river sports, country drives and sociabilities, we mean The Crossmon. The old hotel under the same management as the new, has been referred to. It had been the stopping place for visitors to the islands for more than a quarter of a century and acquired during that time a reputation of which any hotel with similar facilities might be proud. The new, many-towered, Crossmon consists of a five story building, covering exactly the site of the old hotel of pleasant memories. It is a picturesque structure, surrounded by wide verandas and traversed by spacious halls.

THE CROSSMON IN 1848.

THE SITUATION AND OUTLOOK.

It is most charmingly situated, close to the river on the north, and the little gem of a bay from which the village takes its name on the east, thus having *two water sides*. Its windows, verandas and towers afford extensive views of the river and islands in three directions. Most of the prominent islands and cottages may be seen from it, together with miles and miles of the sweeping, bounding, gleaming river. The hotel has in reality two fronts (with their entrances,) the one being toward the river, where boat-passengers enter, and the other on the main village street, where carriages are the mode of conveyance.

PRINCIPAL ADVANTAGES OF THE CROSSMON.

The office, wine room, billiard room and barber shop being on the street front of the hotel, are entirely removed from the water front, where the verandas are, and where the guests like to assemble for games and promenading. An elevator runs from the basement to the top of the building, and the broad stairways in both main building and wing, afford quick means of egress in case of fire.

The hotel is lighted throughout with gas, and supplied with pure river water, which is forced by a steam engine into an enormous *copper tank* on the roof, and conveyed from there to the various floors by means of *galvanized iron pipes*, thus doing away with all danger of *lead poisoning*, and other impurities. On every floor are water-closets and bath-rooms, with hot and cold water. Electrical bells and speaking tubes connect the office with every part of the building. It will accommodate three hundred guests and is adapted to satisfy those who are accustomed to luxurious homes.

THE CROSSMON IN 1863.

The table is supplied with all the delicacies of the season, prepared by accomplished cooks; and the best brand of foreign wines, beers and liquors await the orders of all who desire them.

Morning concerts are given by a fine orchestra, and the amusements of the day are varied in the evening by music, dancing and games in the parlors, and thus the round of enjoyment may be continued from early morning until late bedtime. There are over five hundred feet of verandas, and guests may promenade the entire distance, and through the long halls, without obstruction.

Appetizing lunches are neatly put up free of charge at the hotel, for picnic and fishing parties, and, after a ride on the river, are often enjoyed in the open air, under the trees, even better than the most sumptuous dinners in the dining rooms. Boats, oarsmen and fishing tackle can be engaged for parties wishing them by applying at the hotel office.

The grounds of the hotel, over an acre in extent, have been nicely grassed and graded and are beautified in places by beds of flowers.

On the east, towards the bay, is an extensive lawn, reaching to the water's edge. On this side is the principal landing place for yachts and smaller boats. On the north is a

THE CROSSMON IN 1873.

rocky incline, spotted with grass and flowers. The grounds, as well as the buildings, are brilliantly illuminated at night, colored lights shining in all the towers, which have a peculiarly beautiful effect as seen from the river.

Notwithstanding the extensive accommodations, the Crossmon is crowded much of the time during the warm season, and it is therefore a good plan for parties wishing rooms, to engage them in advance by letter, or through the agency of friends.

Address,

CROSSMON & SON,
THE CROSSMON,
ALEXANDRIA BAY, N. Y

THE CROSSMON IN 1881.

The following are the names of the inhabited island and points beginning in order at Clayton and extending below Alexandria Bay.

GOVERNOR'S—three acres, owned by... ....Hon. T. G. Alvord, Syracuse, N. Y

CALUMET—three acres, owned by.............. ....Chas. G. Emory, New York

LONG ROCK—one acre, owned by.................................W. F. Wilson, Watertown, N. Y

HEMLOCK—twenty acres, owned by............Hon W. F. Porter, W. F. Wilson, Watertown, N. Y., and Hon. Henry Spicer, Perch River.

STEWART, OR JEFFERS—ten acres, owned by ....E. P. Gardiner, Syracuse, N. Y.; John Rogers and Miss Haskell, Carthage, N. Y.; L. J. Burdette, Otsego Camp Club; Caleb Clark, Cooperstown, N. Y.; Miss E. M. Griswold, Adams, N. Y.; Wesley M. Rich, Joseph Sayles, Rome, N. Y.; Reuben Fuller, Chas. Ellis, Clayton, N. Y.; Chas. Chickering, Copenhagen, N. Y.; C. O. Pratt, Syracuse, N. Y.

Two in Eel Bay—two acres, owned by..........................Dr. E. L. Sargent, Watertown, N. Y

TWIN—one acre, owned by....................................J. L. Huntington, Theresa, N. Y

WATCH—one acre, owned by ... .S. F. Skinner, New York

OCCIDENT AND ORIENT—three acres, owned by.......................E. W. Washburne, New York

ISLE OF PINES—two acres, owned by..............................Mrs. E. N. Robinson, New York

FREDERICK'S—two acres, owned by...............................C. L. Frederick, Carthage, N. Y

BAY SIDE—one acre, owned by..................................H. F. Mosher, Watertown, N. Y

RIVER SIDE—(*Main Land*) one acre, owned by ....James C. Lee, Gouverneur, N. Y

KILLEIN'S POINT—(*Main Land*) one acre, owned by.................—— Killien, Lockport, N. Y

HOLLOWAY'S POINT—(*Main Land*) one acre, owned by..............Nathan Holloway, Omar, N. Y

FISHER'S LANDING—(*Main Land*) two acres, owned by.....Mrs. R. Gurnee, Miss Newton, Omar, N. Y

ISLAND HOME—one acre, owned by..............................Mrs. S. D. Hungerford, Adams, N. Y

HARMONY—one-fourth acre, owned by...........................Mrs. Celia Berger, Syracuse, N. Y

Waving Branches—owned by....D. C. Graham, Stone Mills, N. Y.; A. Snell, Lafargeville, N. Y.;
(*Wells Island.*)   J. Petrie, Watertown, N. Y.; Jerome B. Louks, Lafargeville, N. Y.; Isaac
                Mitchell, L. Hughes, Stone Mills, N. Y.; L. Ainsworth, F. Smith, H. S.
                Tolles, Ira Traver, Watertown, N. Y.

Bonny Eyrie—(*Wells Island*) owned by......................................Mrs. Peck, Boonville, N. Y

Throop Dock—(*Wells Island*) owned by..Dr. C. E. Latimer, Watertown, N. Y., and Dr. S. J. Latimer,
                New York City.

Jolly Oaks—(*Wells Island*) two acres, owned by.......Prof. A. H. Brown, Dr. N. D. Ferguson, John
                Norton, O. T. Green,Carthage, N.Y.; Hon. W. W. Butterfield, Redwood, N. Y

——————— —owned by..............................M. Kenyon and Miss Parker, Watertown, N. Y

Calumet—one-half acre, owned by...........................Rev. H. R. Waite, New Rochelle, N. Y

Point Vivian—ten acres, owned by........Rezot Tozer, J. J. Kinney, E. O. Hungerford, Geo. Ivers,
(*Main Land.*)   Evans Mill, N. Y.; and others.

Lindner's—one acre, owned by.... .. .. John Lindner, Jersey City, N. J.

Island Royal—one acre, owned by....................................Royal E. Deane, New York

Cedar—one acre, owned by...J. M. Curtis, Cleveland, Ohio

Wild Rose—one acre, owned by...................................Hon. W. G. Rose, Cleveland, Ohio

Allegheny Point—(*Main Land*) two acres, owned by....................J. S. Laney, Foxburg, Pa

Photo—two acres, owned by.................................... A. C. McIntyre, Brockville, Ont

Seven Isles—five acres, owned by........................Hon. Bradley Winslow, Watertown, N. Y

Louisiana Point—(*Wells Island*) three acres, owned by........Hon. D. C. LaBatt, New Orleans, La

Bella Vista Lodge—(*Main Land*) five acres, owned by.............F. J. Bosworth, Milwaukee, Wis

Nemah-bin—two acres, owned by..............................James H. Oliphant, Brooklyn, N. Y

Comfort—two acres, owned by....................................A. E. Clark, Chicago, Ill

Warner Island—one acre, owned by ....H. H. Warner, Rochester, N. Y

Wau Winet—one-half acre, owned by...C. E. Hill, Chicago, Ill
Cuba—one acre, owned by...Dr. W. E. Story, Buffalo, N. Y
Devil's Oven—one acre, owned by..................................II. R. Heath, Brooklyn, N. Y
Sunny-Side—(Cherry Island) five acres, owned by.............Rev. Geo. H. Rockwell, New York
Melrose Lodge—(Cherry Island) nine acres, owned by..A. B. Pullman and G. B. Marsh, Chicago, Ill
Safe Point—(Wells Island) four acres, owned by.....................II. H. Warner, Rochester, N. Y
Pullman—three acres, owned by....................................Geo. M. Pullman, Chicago, Ill
Nobby—three acres, owned by....................................H. R. Heath, Brooklyn, N. Y
Little Angel—one-eighth acre, owned by............................W. A. Angell, Chicago, Ill
Welcome—three acres, owned by............................Hon. S. G. Pope, Ogdensburg, N. Y
Friendly—three acres, owned by....................A. B. Parker and Abner Mellen, Jr., New York
Linlithgow—one-fourth acre, owned by ....Hon. R. A. Livingston, New York
Florence—two acres, owned by...H. S. Chandler, New York

SUNNYSIDE,

the summer home of Rev. George Rockwell, now of New York City, but best known in this region as for more than twenty years the pastor of the Reformed Church, the first organized at Alexandria Bay.

St. Elmo—three acres, owned by..............................Nathaniel W. Hunt, Brooklyn, N. Y
Felseneck—owned by...Prof. A. G. Hopkins, Clinton, N. Y
Point Lookout—one acre, owned by.............................Miss L. J. Bullock, Adams, N. Y
Cleveland Point—(Main Land) thirty acres, owned by Hon. W. G. Rose and J. M. Curtis Cleveland, O
Edgewood—(Point Main Land) one acre, owned by.................G. C. Martin, Watertown, N. Y
West View—   "   "   "   one acre, owned by.............Hon. S. G. Pope, Ogdensburg, N. Y

VILULA—(*Point Main Land*) half acre, owned by........................H. Sisson, Watertown, N. Y
ISLE IMPERIAL—one acre, owned by........................Mrs. H. G. Le Conte, Philadelphia, Pa
FERN—one acre, owned by........................N. and J. Winslow, Watertown, N. Y
HART'S—five acres, owned by........................Hon. E. K. Hart, Albion, N. Y
DESHLER—fifteen acres, owned by........................W. G. Deshler, Columbus, Ohio
NETTS—one acre, owned by........................Wm. B. Hayden, Columbus, Ohio
BONNIE CASTLE—(*Point Main Land*) fifteen acres, owned by..........Mrs. J. G. Holland, New York
CRESCENT COTTAGES—(*Main Land*) ten acres, owned by..........Bleecker Van Wagenen, New York
POINT MARGUERITE— " " thirty acres, owned by........................E. Anthony, New York
LONG BRANCH—(*Point Main Land*) ten acres, owned by..........Mrs. C. E. Clark, Watertown, N. Y
MANHATTAN—five acres, owned by........................J. L. Hasbrouck and Hon. J. C. Spencer, New York
ST. JOHN'S—six acres, owned by........................Hon. Chas. Donohue, New York
MAPLE—six acres, owned by........................J. L. Hasbrouck, New York
FAIRY LAND—20 acres, owned by Peter C. Hayden, Chas. H. Hayden and Wm. B. Hayden, Columbus, O
LITTLE FRAUD—one-half acre, owned by........................R. Pease, Geneva, N. Y
HUGUENOT—two acres, owned by........................Levi Hasbrouck, Ogdensburg, N. Y
RESORT—three acres, owned by........................Cornwall Bros., Alexandria Bay, N. Y
DEER—forty acres, owned by........................Hon. S. Miller, New Haven, Conn
ISLAND MARY—two acres, owned by........................Wm. L. Palmer, Carthage, Dak
WALTON—seven acres, owned by........................J. N. Robbins and G. H. Robinson, New York
IDLEWILD—four acres, owned by........................Mrs. R. A. Packer, Sayre, Pa
LITTLE LEHIGH—one acre, owned by........................Chas. H. Cummings, New York
SPORT—four acres, owned by........................Mrs. H. E. Packer, Mauch Chunk, Pa
SUNNY-SIDE—two acres, owned by........................W. Stevenson, Sayre, Pa
SUMMER-LAND—ten acres........................Summer-Land Association
   "Summer-Land" is owned by the "Summer-Land Association," composed of the following
   members: Rev. Asa Saxe, D. D., Francis M. McFarlin, James Sargeant, Emory B. Chase,
   Lean E. Brace, Isaiah F. Force, Henry C. Wisner, Lewis P. Ross, Charles W. Gray,
   George A. Newell, Henry O. Hall, Joseph A. Stud and Frank W. Hawley, of Rochester,
   N. Y.; Rev. Almon Gunnison, D. D., and Frank Sperry, of Brooklyn; Rev. Richmond
   Fisk, Alfred Underhill and Horace Bronson, of Syracuse, N. Y.

ARCADIA AND INA—five acres, owned by........................S. A. Briggs, New York
SPUYTEN DUYVEL—one acre, owned by........................Alice P. Sargent, New York
DOUGLAS—five acres, owned by........................Douglas Miller, New Haven, Conn
KIT GRAFTON—one-half acre, owned by........................Mrs. S. L. George, Watertown, N. Y
LOOKOUT—two acres, owned by........................Thomas H. Borden, New York
ELLA—one-fourth acre, owned by........................R. E. Hungerford, Watertown, N. Y
LITTLE CHARM—one-eighth acre, owned by........................Mrs. F. W. Barker, Alexandria Bay, N. Y
FROST—two acres, owned by........................Mrs. S. L. Frost, Watertown, N. Y
EXCELSIOR GROUP—five acres, owned by........................C. S. Goodwin, New York
SYLVAN AND MOSS—three acres, owned by........................S. T. Woolworth, Watertown N. Y
ELEPHANT ROCK—one-eighth acre, owned by........................T. C. Chittenden, Watertown, N. Y
SUNBEAM GROUP—one acre, owned by........................C. E. Alling, Rochester, N. Y
ALICE—two acres, owned by........................Col. A. J. Casse, New York
SCHOONER—six acres, owned by........................J. Norman Whitehouse, New York
BIRCH—seven acres, owned by........................W. J. Lewis, Pittsburgh, Pa
OURS—three acres, owned by........................Mrs. M. Carter, Poughkeepsie, N. Y
BERKSHIRE—twenty acres, owned by........................Hon. S. G. Pope, Ogdensburg, N. Y

Dedicated to the Guests of The Crossmon.

ON THE ST. LAWRENCE.

By GEORGE C. BRAGDON.

AWAY! away! the golden day
 Beams brightly on the river,
And time beguils where happy isles
Rest peacefully forever;
 And smilingly forever,
 Invitingly forever.

Where isles of green o'erlook the sheen
 Of fair St. Lawrence river,
The silver sheen round isles of green,
 Upon St. Lawrence river.

Ah! fair the isles, adorned with smiles
 To greet the wooing river;
We float between, 'neath branches green,
 And long to float forever,
 To dream and float forever,
 Forgetfully forever.

With line and boat to dream and float
 On blue St. Lawrence river,
To dream and float with line and boat
 Adown St. Lawrence river.

IN THE REEDS NEAR WELLS ISLAND.

Now dipping oar recedes the shore,
 And on the restless river
We gaily ride, we bound and glide,
 While sunbeams flash and quiver,
 Around us flash and quiver
 From billows flash and quiver.

And all is bright and care is light
 On old St. Lawrence river,
And care is light, and all is bright
 Upon St. Lawrence River.

Shall we forget the friends we met
 And loved upon the river?—
Its songs and dreams and changing gleams?
 No, never, and no never,
 We shall forget them never,
 We can forget them never.

The thousand joys and sweet alloys,
 Of dear St. Lawrence river,
With sweet alloys the thousand joys
 Of Thousand Island River.

ROUTES TO THE BAY.

Leave the N. Y. Central at Rome, and enter the palace cars of the Rome, Watertown & Ogdensburg Railroad. A few hours ride on these will bring you to Cape Vincent, thirty miles from Alexandria Bay, where steamers run to and fro twice a day, connecting closely with the trains.

Take the West Shore route via Utica in connection with Utica and Black River Railroad, or via Syracuse in connection with the Rome, Watertown and Ogdensburg Railroad.

Or if you please take the other branch at Watertown, and ride through a picturesque country to Ogdensburg, (six hours from Rome,) and there take steamer up the river to the Bay, 36 miles.

Or leave the Central at Syracuse (which shortens the distance for parties from the west,) and take the Syracuse Northern to Richland, from which place the route is again on the R. W. & O. R. R.

Or starting from Oswego (to which city is a railroad from Syracuse and lines of steamers from all the principal points of the great lakes, some of which go to the Bay,) a branch of the R. W. & O. connects with the main road to Richland.

Or if from the east, you take the Delaware & Hudson at Troy, or Albany, going through Saratoga and along the west shore of Lake Champlain, to Rouses Pt., there taking the Ogdensburg & Lake Champlain R. R. to Ogdensburg, having a delightful sail from Ogdensburg by steamer to Alexandria Bay.

Or leaving Albany or Troy via. D. & H. C. Co., taking steamers through Lakes George and Champlain, (the most delightful of all,) to Plattsburgh, D. & H. to Rouses Point, O. & L. C., and steamer to Alexandria Bay, making one of the best trips in this country.

Or you can leave the Central at Utica and take the cars on Utica & Black River R. R., which will carry you without change of cars to Clayton, in four and a half hours, 12 miles from Alexandria Bay, where a steamer will be found which will complete the journey in one hour.

Or from Chicago and the west you can take the first limited Express via. Chicago & Grand Trunk R. R. at 3:20 P. M. daily, with through Pullman Sleepers for Boston, arriving at Alexandria Bay the next evening in time for supper, via. steamer from Kingston, 25 miles distance. The "boss" route.

Or from Portland, Old Orchard Beach, Montreal and Quebec and Maine resorts, take the Grand Trunk R. R. to Brockville, Gananoque or Kingston, and steamers from those points to Alexandria Bay, making one of the most delightful trips in this country.

Or starting from New York, take the New York, Ontario and Western R. R. from West 42d St., Cortlandt or Desbrosses Sts. ferries, and enter the through Pullman Buffet Sleeping Cars for Cape Vincent; (this is the only route from New York running Pullman Sleepers to the islands.)

At Cape Vincent the new Steamer St. Lawrence makes close connection with the trains, running thirty miles down the river, through the islands to the Bay.

Connections with the Pennsylvania R. R. by this route are made at Jersey City in Union Station, and all transfer across New York City avoided.

From Portland, Old Orchard Beach, and Maine resorts, take the Portland & Ogdensburg R. R., passing through the White Mountains and Vermont via. Rouses Point to Ogdensburg, and steamer to Alexandria Bay. This is the shortest line from the White Mountains and Maine.

The U. & B. R. R. R. has been completed to Ogdensburg, from which point steamers also run to the Bay. A four-horse coach will run from Redwood station to the Bay, seven miles, connecting with the trains.

Visitors from the east whose route is by the Northern Railroad, which connects with the Vermont Central, will take a steamer at Ogdensburg for the rest of the journey, which leaves upon the arrival of train, reaching the Bay in time for supper.

The Royal Mail line of steamers run from Niagara Falls to Montreal, passing down the St. Lawrence by daylight, and stopping at the Bay.

Since the completion of the Lake Ontario Shore Railroad, facilities for reaching Alexandria Bay from the west have improved. Parties may now leave Niagara Falls in Palace cars in the morning and ride in them to Cape Vincent, and there taking a steamer, arrive at the Bay in time for supper.

HOTELS EN ROUTE.

The following hotels, among others, are recommended to persons en route to the Thousand Islands, on account of their accommodations and management :—

BAGG'S HOTEL, Utica, N. Y..T. R. Proctor, Proprietor
GLOBE HOTEL, Syracuse, N. Y....................................Dickenson & Austin, Proprietors
POWERS HOTEL, Rochester, N. Y.............. ....Buck & Sanger, Proprietors
OSBURNE HOUSE, Auburn, N. Y.............. ....J. E. Allen, Proprietor
SEYMOUR HOUSE, Ogdensburg, N. Y.....................................F. J. Tallman, Proprietor
DANIELS HOTEL, Prescott, Ont...L. H. Daniels, Proprietor
RUSSELL HOUSE, Ottawa, Ont.................................... ...James Guin, Proprietor
ST. LAWRENCE HALL, Montreal, Que.......................................H. Hogan, Proprietor
FOQUET'S HOTEL, Plattsburgh, N. Y.....................................A. J. Sweet, Proprietor
FERGUSON HOUSE, Malone, N. Y.....................................S. E. Flanagan, Proprietor
WINDSOR HOTEL, Montreal....................................Geo. W. Swett, Proprietor
SPRING HOUSE, Richfield Springs....................................T. R. Proctor, Proprietor

DISTANCE CARD.

Niagara to Toronto...................	.40 Miles	Montreal to New York.................	.406 Miles
Toronto to Alexandria Bay........ ....167 "		" " Albany	.251 "
Oswego to Alexandria Bay ....100 "		" " Troy......................	.251 "
Clayton to Alexandria Bay.... . ....12 "		" " Saratoga..................	.212 "
Alexandria Bay to Montreal.......169 "		" " White Mountains	.201 "
" " Watertown..........28 "		Ogdensburg to Ottawa..................	.53 "
" " Utica.............132 "		Montreal to Quebec	.180 "
" " Brockville...........24 "		Ogdensburg to Malone	.61 "
" " Portland, via O. & L. C. 400 "		" " Chateaugay	.73 "
" " Boston, via O. & L. C..442 "		" " Chateaugay Chasm......74½ "
" " Ogdensburg ....36 "		" " Ralph's................	.88 "
Montreal to Portland.................278 "		" " Saratoga... ....255 "

1885. SEASON. **1885.**

ROME, WATERTOWN & OGDENSBURG RAILROAD.

THE DIRECT ROUTE FROM ALL POINTS

South, West and East,

—— TO ——

CAPE VINCENT, CLAYTON, ALEXANDRIA BAY

—— AND ——

✤ THE THOUSAND ISLANDS ✤

OF THE

Majestic River St. Lawrence.

THROUGH

Express-Trains, with THROUGH COACHES, *Sleeping and Drawing-Room Cars attached*, will run Daily (Sundays excepted,) between Rome, Syracuse and Niagara Falls, and Cape Vincent, where direct connections are made with the *New and Fast Steel-plate Side-wheel Steamer "ST. LAWRENCE,"* making two trips daily (Sundays excepted,) between *Cape Vincent and Alexandria Bay,* stopping at Clayton, Round Island, Thousand Island and Central Parks, and connecting at Alexandria Bay with Ferry for Westminster Park.

This NEW and FAST Steamer, with capacity for carrying one thousand people, was built the past year expressly for this route, and is specially adapted for sight-seeing and the

ACCOMMODATION AND COMFORT OF PLEASURE TRAVEL,

Has an Elegant Cabin, State Rooms, and a large covered Promenade Deck. Also facilities for serving meals, which will be **First Class** and at moderate prices. The finishing and furnishing is complete in every particular, thus affording advantages and comforts that can not be enjoyed BY ANY OTHER ROUTE.

ST. LAWRENCE STEAMBOAT EXPRESS,

With THROUGH SLEEPING-CAR attached, will leave Niagara Falls daily (Saturdays excepted,) about 7 P. M., and run through, via Philadelphia and U. & B. R. RR., to Clayton, making direct and close connections with the

AMERICAN LINE OF PALACE DAY STEAMERS

For MONTREAL, passing the Thousand Islands and descending all the Rapids by daylight.

EXCURSION OR TOURISTS' TICKETS

May be obtained of this Company's Agents and at all principal offices of connecting lines EAST, WEST and SOUTH. Rates as low and time as quick as via any other route.

This Company have lately added

STEEL RAILS ! NEW COACHES ! **WESTINGHOUSE AUTOMATIC AIR BRAKES !**
MILLER'S PATENT PLATFORMS AND COUPLERS !

And all the modern appliances for the safety and comfort of passengers, making this the *most desirable Route* for tourists and pleasure seekers.

BE SURE AND SECURE TICKETS READING VIA THE **POPULAR LINE.**

H. M. BRITTON,
General Manager.

E. M. MOORE,
General Passenger Agent.

THE MOST DIRECT,

AND BY FAR THE MOST ATTRACTIVE ROUTE

—— BETWEEN ——

THE EASTERN COAST, THE WHITE MOUNTAIN RESORTS, AND

ALEXANDRIA BAY AND THE THOUSAND ISLANDS,

—— IS VIA THE ——

PORTLAND & OGDENSBURG RAILROAD

AND ITS CONNECTIONS.

Daily Train Service, during the Pleasure Season, between

PORTLAND, MAINE, and OGDENSBURG, N. Y.,

In well appointed cars, over good track, and through the finest scenery on the Continent.

The Route is through the famous

NOTCH OF THE WHITE MOUNTAINS,

Across Vermont, skirting the beautiful Green Mountain Range, bridging Lake Champlain at Rouse's Point, and thence over the O. & L. C. RR. to Ogdensburg, where connection is made with all points in the Thousand Islands district.

At Portland, connection is made with all lines from Boston, the principal Beach Resorts,

OLD ORCHARD, MT. DESERT, AND THE PROVINCES,

And at Norwood and Ogdensburg with through lines to and from Syracuse, Niagara Falls,
☞ AND ALL POINTS WEST. ☜

Tourists Eastbound, via the St. Lawrence River and Montreal, should
take trains leaving Montreal via

South Eastern Railway or Central Vermont Railroad,

Connecting with P. &. O. RR., by which routes only can they conveniently and at
least expense reach the principal WHITE MOUNTAIN Resorts,
as well as the Watering-Places of the Coast.

Through tickets to Portland and East may be obtained at principal offices of R , W. & O.,
U. & B. R., N. Y. C. & H. R., and their Western connections, and at ticket
offices of P. & O. RR. Return tickets may be had for
Montreal, Ogdensburg, Niagara Falls,
AND ALL POINTS WEST.

Letters of inquiry addressed to General Ticket Office will be promptly answered.

CHAS. H, FRYE, G. T. A.   J. HAMILTON, Supt.

OFFICES AT PORTLAND, ME.

THE MISSOURI PACIFIC RAILWAY COMPANY.

The Missouri Pacific Railway, St. Louis, Iron Mountain & Southern Railway, Central Branch U. P. R. R.
Texas & Pacific Railway, Missouri, Kansas & Texas Railway, International and Great
Northern Railroad, Galveston, Houston & Henderson Railroad.

TOTAL MILEAGE 6029 MILES.

THE DIRECT ROUTE FROM

ST. LOUIS, HANNIBAL, CAIRO, MEMPHIS, GALVESTON

AND NEW ORLEANS,

——TO ALL POINTS IN——

MISSOURI, KANSAS, NEBRASKA, COLORADO, WYOMING, UTAH, ARKANSAS, INDIAN
TERRITORY, TEXAS, ARIZONA, NEW & OLD MEXICO, CALIFORNIA.

PULLMAN PALACE, HOTEL BUFFET AND SLEEPING CARS.

PALACE RECLINING CHAIR CARS.

GEO. OLDS, General Traffic Manager,
ST. LOUIS, MO.

H. C. TOWNSEND, Gen'l Pass. & Ticket Ag't,
ST. LOUIS, MO.

H. C. CHAPMAN,   J. P. McCANN,   E. M. NEWBEGIN,   A. H. TORRICELLI,
Contracting Ag't,   Trav. Pass. Ag't,   Trav. Pass. Ag't,   New England Agt.,
243 BROADWAY, N. Y.   214 WASHINGTON St., BOSTON, Mass.

W. F. TOWNE, General Eastern Agent.   Wm. E HOYT, Eastern Passenger Agent,
243 BROADWAY, NEW YORK.

TRENTON FALLS AND MOORE'S HOTEL.

TRENTON FALLS,

Situated on the line of the U. & B. R. RR., 18 miles from Utica and 102 miles from Alexandria Bay, is one of the Most Delightful of Summer Resorts. The romantic beauty of the place, with its rock-bound and tree-embowered stream, its rushing and picturesque falls, its retired and shady walks, is unsurpassed. Besides, the air and water there are the purest. It is reached by a few minutes' ride from Utica on the cars, and it has a Hotel of National **REPUTATION**.

MOORE'S HOTEL

is a very spacious three story building, with long and wide piazzas, attractive rooms, and a most genial and accomplished host. The Hotel has a front of 136 feet, piazza 12 feet wide, a dining-room 60 by 30 feet, large and well ventilated suites of rooms, a table supplied with all the dainties of the season, served in the best style—in fact, all the **Luxuries** of a

FIRST CLASS WATERING-PLACE HOTEL.

Mr. Moore has been to great trouble and expense in building stairways, laying out the beautiful grounds, and making arrangements for perfect security in visiting the wild falls and chasms of the stream. His Hotel is also

AN ART GALLERY OF GREAT INTEREST.

TOURISTS AND PLEASURE SEEKERS SHOULD NOT OVERLOOK THIS CHARMING SUMMER RESORT.

Passengers en route to or from Alexandria Bay, via Utica & Black River RR., have the privilege of stopping off at Trenton Falls, and resuming the trip at their pleasure.

STEAMER ISLAND WANDERER.

DESCRIPTIVE TIME TABLE.

The Steamer Island Wanderer on her Forty Mile Trip Among the Islands.

Leaving Alexandria Bay at 8:00 A. M. and 2:15 P. M., passing Friendly Island, Nobby Island, Cherry Island, Pullman Island, Wauwinett Island, Warner Island, Devil's Oven, Louisiana Point, reaching Thousand Island Park at 8:40 A. M. and 2:55 P. M., Round Island Park 9:00 A. M. Then passing many miles among

The Green Decked Isles

crossing the boundary line between the United States and Canada, passing Lake Island, Quarry Island. Hay Island, and hundreds of others of less historic note. We reach Gananoque, Ont., at 10 A. M. and 4:00 P. M., stopping 25 minutes in the afternoon for a stroll in Canada. Thence we pass

Down the Canada Water,

going among large groups of the most beautiful islands in the grand old St. Lawrence, which has heretofore never been explored by a large steamer, nor has eye ever gazed upon from a steamer's deck. Also rounding the noted Fiddler's Elbow and passing through

The Lost Channel

(the most interesting feature of the trip,) we enter the main channel of the Canadian waters, passing close to Echo Point, reaching Westminster Park at 11 A. M. and 5 P. M. From here we pass close to Sport Island, Hayden's Island, St. John's Island, Long Branch, Manhattan Group, Anthony Point, Bonnie Castle, Hart's Island, Imperial Island, reaching Alexandria Bay in time for dinner and tea, 12 noon, and 6 P. M. We also leave Alexandria Bay at 12 noon, for Thousand Island Park and Round Island Park and return, and again at 6:00 P.M. for Thousand Island Park and return.

THE STEAMER ISLAND WANDERER is the only boat that makes this trip regular twice daily through the season (Sundays excepted.) Leaving Alexandria Bay Sundays at 3:00 P. M., returning at 6:00 P. M.

Maps of the River and Route, also descriptive books, may be found with our Ticket Agents at Cornwall Bros. and Thousand Island House News Stand, Alexandria Bay, R. A. Irving, Thousand Island Park, Hotel Round Island Park, Charles Brittan, Gananoque, Hotel Westminster Park, and on board the Steamer at News Stand.

FARE, ROUND TRIP FROM ANY POINT 50 CENTS.

E. W. VISGER, Captain.

NEW YORK, ONTARIO AND WESTERN RAILWAY CO.

ONTARIO ROUTE.

SEASON========OF========1885.

THROUGH

PULLMAN PALACE BUFFET SLEEPING CARS

BETWEEN NEW YORK AND THE THOUSAND ISLANDS.

ALL RAIL. DIRECT ROUTE.

This is the only ALL RAIL ROUTE running through **PULLMAN SLEEPING CARS** without change from New York to the Islands. Connecting at Cape Vincent with the new Palace Steamer St. Lawrence, running down through the Islands to Alexandria Bay.

Always on Time. No Change of Cars.

The Pullman Buffet Sleepers run on this line are of the latest model, and are the most magnificent cars put in the public service.

All passengers via this route make connection in Union Depot at Jersey City with the trains of the Pennsylvania Railroad for Newark, Trenton, Philadelphia, Washington and the West, avoiding transfer across New York City.

BREAKFAST AT RICHLAND.

Thousand Island Express leaves New York, 42nd st. depot 5:40 P. M., Cortland and Desbrosses st. 5:30 P. M., arriving at Cape Vincent 10:35 A. M., and at Alexandria Bay, via Steamer St. Lawrence at 12:30 P. M.—running twenty-five miles down the river through the entire length of the Thousand Islands.

New York Express leaves Alexandria Bay via Steamer St. Lawrence at 1:10 P. M., leave Cape Vincent at 4:00 P. M., arrives at New York at 10:00 A. M. Through Pullman Sleeping Cars between Cape Vincent and New York.

All trains via the "Ontario Route" run along the picturesque West Shore of the Hudson, through the Highlands, over the foot hills of the Catskills and through the mountain regions of Central New York, as well as through the beautiful valleys of the Delaware, Susquehanna and Chenango Rivers, making the landscape route across the Empire State.

TOURISTS' TICKETS ON SALE AT ALL OFFICES,

embracing trips to Niagara Falls, Lake Regions of Canada, Thousand Islands, Montreal, Quebec, Lake Champlain, White Mountains, etc., etc.

Time Tables, Tickets and Information Furnished at any of the Company's Offices Below.

In Weehaken—N. Y. O. & Western Station. In Hoboken—Nos. 115 & 254 Washington street. In Jersey City—Pennsylvania Railroad Station. In Brooklyn—No 4 Court street, No. 7 DeKalb Avenue, No. 838 Fulton street, No. 860 Fulton street, Brooklyn Annex office, foot of Fulton street. 107 Broadway, Williamsburgh, 210 Manhattan Ave., Greenport. In New York City—No. 363 Broadway, corner Franklin street, No. 397 Broadway, No. 946 Broadway, near Madison Square, No. 737 Sixth Avenue, corner of 42d street, No. 1333 Broadway, near 33d street, No. 421 Broadway, corner Canal, No. 168 East 125th street, Harlem. Astor House Ticket Office, No. 207 Broadway, World Travel Company, No. 261 Broadway, Thos. Cook & Son, Tourist Office, No. 5 Union Square, Leve & Alden, Tourist Office, Pennsylvania Railroad Station, foot of Desbrosses street, Pennsylvania Railroad Station, foot of Cortlandt street, N. Y., O. & W. R'y, foot of West 42d street. In Philadelphia—Corner Broad and Chestnut sts., Leve & Alden, Tourist Office.

Agents of the New York Transfer Company, New York, will furnish tickets, and check baggage from residence to destination.

Send for a copy of "Summer Homes" along the New York, Ontario & Western Railway, with full list of Summer Hotels, Boarding Houses, terms, etc. This book is replete with valuable information, and is furnished free on application.

J. E. CHILDS, Gen'l Supt.   **J. C. ANDERSON, Gen'l Passenger Ag't.**
MILLS BUILDING, 15 BROAD ST., NEW YORK.

CENTENNIAL HALL,

One of the most attractive features at Alexandria Bay is Centennial Hall. It is a magnificent structure in the style of a Swiss cottage, 60x14 feet in size, entirely surrounded by a broad veranda 8½ feet wide, making the entire dimensions 77x31 feet: thus affording a delightful uninterrupted promenade of 216 feet.

The entire finishing and furnishing is of the richest description. Its sides are made up of windows, from each of which is a fine view. At each end are windows of stained glass. Flagstaffs surmount the edifice, bearing the respective banners of the United States and England. Well, you ask, what is all this for? Just what we are coming at. Here will be kept

ALL THE DELICACIES OF THE SEASON.

Here you will find the most delicious of ice creams, made of *cream*, too, my dear madam. Think of an iced lemonade in this delightful spot! Perhaps it is some of those fresh tempting oranges, pineapples, peaches or bananas that you prefer. If it be anything in the line of fruits, or the most tempting of confectionery, they are here. Here, too, is the

CHOICEST LITERATURE OF THE DAY.

Books, papers, magazines, etc., and McIntyre's Gems of the Thousand Isles are had here, and in fact much of all that goes to make life pleasant as well as profitable. In a word, Centennial Hall is *un Grand Place du Resort*.

DO NOT FAIL TO VISIT IT.

We grow hundreds of kinds of **FLOWER AND VEGETABLE SEEDS,** and import from the most renowned growers in the world. We design to keep the best seeds in the world, and the most complete assortment of everything worthy of culture.

We also publish the following works :

A beautiful Horticultural Magazine, published monthly. Each number contains a handsome Colored plate, 32 pages of reading matter, and many fine Wood Cuts. It has several departments.

EDITORIAL, containing articles on leading Horticultural subjects, with fine illustrations.

CORRESPONDENCE: Each number has interesting communications from every section of the country, while from time to time we are favored with valuable contributions from over the ocean.

FOREIGN NOTES is an interesting department, as it contains the latest garden notes from foreign journals.

PLEASANT GOSSIP: In this section practical answers are given to questions that daily arise in plant and garden culture, and much information is imparted in a plain and pleasant way.

OUR YOUNG PEOPLE is entertaining, instructive, and fully illustrated.

Price $1.25 a year ; five copies $5.00.

VICK'S FLORAL GUIDE

A BEAUTIFUL WORK OF .

Over One Hundred Pages,

One Colored Flower-Plate,

and 1000 Illustrations

with descriptions of the best Flowers and Vegetables, with prices of seeds, and how to grow them. All for 10 cents. In English or German.

VICK'S

FLOWER AND VEGETABLE GARDEN,

Revised and Enlarged,

CONTAINING

Two Hundred and Ten Pages,

SIX COLORED PLATES,

and many hundred Engravings. In elegant cloth $1.25.

ADDRESS JAMES VICK, ROCHESTER, N. Y.

1848.　The Old Established Route.　1885.

OGDENSBURG & LAKE CHAMPLAIN RAILROAD,

THE MOST DIRECT LINE BETWEEN

Alexandria Bay, Thousand Islands,

—AND—

New York, New Haven, Hartford, Providence, Worcester, Troy, Albany, Saratoga, Boston, Lowell, Lawrence, Nashua, Portland, White Mountains, Old Orchard Beach, Mt. Desert,

—AND—

THE ADIRONDACK WILDERNESS,

Via the Great Natural Highways,

MALONE AND CHATEAUGAY.

THE ONLY LINE RUNNING IN DIRECT CONNECTION WITH LAKES CHAMPLAIN AND GEORGE STEAMBOATS.

PIONEER CROSSING—POINT LOOKOUT.

VIEWS OF CHATEAUGAY CHASM SCENERY.

GIANT GORGE—PULPIT ROCK.

WONDERFUL FREAKS OF NATURE.

SPARTAN PASS—RAINBOW FALLS.

OGDENSBURG & LAKE CHAMPLAIN RAILROAD.